University of the
West of England
BRISTOL

REDLAND
LIBRARY

This book should be returned by the last date stamped below.

31-JUL96

25. OCT 1996

26. FEB 2004

BRISTOL UWE     B1084/10/92
Printing & Stationery Services

# The Wreck of the *Zephyr*

Written and Illustrated by

CHRIS VAN ALLSBURG

Andersen Press · London
Hutchinson of Australia

**British Library Cataloguing in Publication Data**
Van Allsburg, Chris
  The wreck of the Zephyr
  I. Title
  813'.54[J]      PZ7

ISBN 0-86264-063-6

© 1983 by Chris Van Allsburg. Published in Great Britain in 1984 by Andersen Press Ltd.,
19–21 Conway Street, London W.1. Published in Australia by Hutchinson Publishing Group
(Australia) Pty. Ltd., Hawthorne, Victoria 3122. All rights reserved. Published in the United
States by Houghton Mifflin Company, Boston. Printed in Italy by Grafiche AZ, Verona.

To C. E. Stevens

Once, while travelling along the seashore, I stopped at a small fishing village. After eating lunch, I decided to take a walk. I followed a path out of the village and uphill to some cliffs high above the sea. At the edge of these cliffs was a most unusual sight — the wreck of a small sailing boat.

An old man was sitting among the broken timbers, smoking a pipe. He seemed to be reading my mind when he said, "Odd, isn't it?"

"Yes," I answered. "How did it get here?"

"Waves carried it up during a storm."

"Really?" I said. "It doesn't seem the waves could ever get that high."

The old man smiled. "Well, there is another story." He invited me to have a seat and listen to his strange tale.

"In our village, years ago," he said, "there was a boy who could sail a boat better than any man in the harbour. He could find a breeze over the flattest sea. When dark clouds kept other boats at anchor, the boy would sail out, ready to prove to the villagers, to the sea itself, how great a sailor he was.

"One morning, under an ominous sky, he prepared to take his boat, the *Zephyr*, out to sea. A fisherman warned the boy to stay in port. Already a strong wind was blowing. 'I'm not afraid,' the boy said, 'because I'm the greatest sailor there is.' The fisherman pointed to a sea gull gliding overhead. 'There's the only sailor who can go out on a day like this.' The boy just laughed as he hoisted his sails into a blustery wind.

"The wind whistled in the rigging as the *Zephyr* pounded her way through the water. The sky grew black and the waves rose up like mountains. The boy struggled to keep his boat from going over. Suddenly a gust of wind caught the sail. The boom swung around and hit the boy's head. He fell to the cockpit floor and did not move.

"When the boy opened his eyes, he found himself lying on a beach. The *Zephyr* rested behind him, carried there by the storm. The boat was far from the water's edge. The tide would not carry it back to sea. The boy set out to look for help.

"He walked for a long time and was surprised that he didn't recognize the shoreline. He climbed a hill, expecting to see something familiar, but what he saw instead was a strange and unbelievable sight. Before him were two boats, sailing high above the water. Astonished, he watched them glide by. Then a third sailed past, towing the *Zephyr*. The boats entered a bay that was bordered by a large village. There they left the *Zephyr*.

"The boy made his way down to the harbour, to the dock where his boat was tied. A sailor was there who smiled when he saw the boy. Pointing to the *Zephyr* he asked, 'Yours?' The boy nodded. The sailor said they almost never saw strangers on their island. It was surrounded by a treacherous reef. The *Zephyr* must have been carried over the reef by the storm. He told the boy that, later, they would take him and the *Zephyr* back over the reef. But the boy said he would not leave until he learned to sail above the waves. The sailor told him it took years to learn to sail like that. 'Besides,' he said, 'the *Zephyr* does not have the right sails.' The boy insisted. He pleaded with the sailor.

"Finally the sailor said he would try to teach him if the boy promised to leave the next morning. The boy agreed. The sailor went to a shed and got a new set of sails.

"All afternoon they sailed back and forth across the bay. Sometimes the sailor took the tiller, and the boat would magically begin to lift out of the water. But when the boy tried, he could not catch the wind that made boats fly.

"When the sun went down they went back to the harbour. They dropped anchor and a fisherman rowed them to shore. 'In the morning,' the sailor said, 'we'll put your own sails back on the *Zephyr* and send you home.' He took the boy to his house, and the sailor's wife fed them oyster stew.

"After dinner the sailor played the concertina. He sang a song about a man named Samuel Blue, who, long ago, had tried to sail his boat over land and had crashed:

*'For the wind o'er land's ne'er steady nor true,*
*an' all men that sail there'll meet Samuel Blue.'*

"When he was done with his song, the sailor sent the boy to bed. But the boy could not sleep. He knew he could fly his boat if he had another chance. He waited until the sailor and his wife were asleep, then he quietly dressed and went to the harbour. As he rowed out to the *Zephyr*, the boy felt the light evening wind grow stronger and colder.

"Under a full moon, he sailed the *Zephyr* into the bay. He tried to remember everything the sailor had told him. He tried to feel the wind pulling his boat forward, lifting it up. Then, suddenly, the boy felt the *Zephyr* begin to shake. The sound of the water rushing past the hull grew louder. The air filled with spray as the boat sliced through the waves. The bow slowly began to lift. Higher and higher the *Zephyr* rose out of the water, then finally broke free. The sound of rushing water stopped. There was only the sound of wind in the sails. The *Zephyr* was flying.

"Using the stars to guide him, the boy set a course for home. The wind blew very hard, churning the sea below. But that did not matter to the *Zephyr* as she glided through the night sky. When clouds blocked the boy's view of the stars, he trimmed the sails and climbed higher. Surely the men of the island never dared fly so high. Now the boy was certain he was truly the greatest sailor of all.

"He steered well. Before the night was over, he saw the moonlit spire of the church at the edge of his village. As he drew closer to land, an idea took hold of him. He would sail over the village and ring the *Zephyr*'s bell. Then everyone would see him and know that he was the greatest sailor. He flew over the tree-topped cliffs of the shore, but as he reached the church the *Zephyr* began to fall.

"The wind had shifted. The boy pulled as hard as he could on the tiller, but it did no good. The wind shifted again. He steered for the open sea, but the trees at the cliff's edge stood between him and the water. At first there was just the rustle of leaves brushing the hull. Then the air was filled with the sound of breaking branches and ripping sails. The boat fell to the ground. And here she sits today."

"A remarkable tale," I said, as the old man stopped to relight his pipe. "What happened to the boy?"

"He broke his leg that night. Of course, no one believed his story about flying boats. It was easier for them to believe that he was lost in the storm and thrown up here by the waves." The old man laughed.

"No sir, the boy never amounted to much. People thought he was crazy. He just took odd jobs around the harbour. Most of the time he was out sailing, searching for that island and a new set of sails."

A light breeze blew through the trees. The old man looked up. "Wind coming," he said. "I've got some sailing to do." He picked up a cane, and I watched as he limped slowly towards the harbour.